Hans Christian Andersen

Classic Fairy Tales

Illustrated by
MICHAEL ADAMS

The Unicorn Publishing House
New Jersey

THE FIR TREE

F ar out in the forest, where the sun and the fresh air made a sweet resting-place, grew a pretty little fir-tree. And yet it was not happy, for it wished so much to be tall like the pines and firs which grew around it. "Oh, how I wish I were as tall as the other trees; I would spread out my branches on every side, and my top would overlook the whole wide world." And yet all the while it complained, it was growing.

In the fall, the wood-cutters came and cut down the tallest trees, and the little fir-tree would ask, "Where are they going? What would become of them?" A stork happened by one day and told the little tree that the tall firs where made into masts for ships to sail the open seas. "Oh, how I wish I were tall enough to go on the open seas," the little tree said, though it had not the slightest idea what a ship was or a sea.

"Rejoice in thy youth," said the sunbeam; "rejoice in thy fresh growth, and the young life within you." And the wind kissed the tree, and the dew watered it with tears; but the fir-tree regarded them not.

Three years passed, and the fir-tree grew to its full height, yet it was still unhappy. Christmas-time was near, and the young tree saw people coming into the wood and cutting down trees that were exactly his size. "Where are they going?" asked the fir-tree. "They are not taller than I am: indeed, one is much less. And why are the branches not cut off? Where are they going?"

"We know, we know," sang the sparrows; "we have looked in at the windows of their houses. They dress up the trees in the most splendid manner. They put lights and tiny cakes and beautiful colored apples on their branches."

"And then," asked the fir-tree, trembling through all its branches, "and then what happens?"

"We did not see any more," said the sparrows.

"I wonder whether anything so wonderful will happen to me," thought the fir-tree. "It must be even better than going to sea."

"Rejoice with us," said the air and the sunlight. "Enjoy your own bright life with us in the wood. Rejoice, little tree, in all the good things you have." But the tree would not rejoice.

Then one day, people did come for the little tree. With a groan the fir-tree fell to the earth. It was loaded into a cart and carried away—forever from the woodland home that it knew.

The fir-tree was brought into a home and placed in a large tub. Then children gathered around and put bright ribbons, candy, and oh! a hundred tiny candles on its branches. How beautiful everything was! How wonderful that night! as the children danced around the little tree, laughing and singing. The tree trembled with joy as the children rustled under its branches for the presents placed beneath.

Then, Christmas was past. The decorations were taken down and the fir-tree was dragged, quite roughly, upstairs to the attic. There the tree remained throughout the winter, and it wondered when, oh, when would they dress it up in such finery again.

Spring came, and the attic door flew open. "Now I shall live," cried the tree, joyfully spreading out its branches. But no, they were all withered and yellow and stiff. The fir-tree was dragged back downstairs and taken outside to be burned.

"Past! Past!" said the old tree. "Oh, had I but enjoyed myself while I could have done so! But now it is too late." The tree quickly blazed up, and the sound of its sighs rose in the air. With each "pop, pop," from the tree, which is a deep sigh, it remembered the summer days in the forest, the woodland animals, the sun, the wind, and the children dancing and laughing. Now all was past; the tree's life was past, and the story also— for all stories must come to an end at last.

THE CANDLE

There was once a tallow candle, a very common sort really, the kind you would find in most kitchens. Now this candle lived with a very poor family, but from its place by the kitchen window, it could look across the street and see into the home of a very rich and comfortable family. It was Christmas Eve, and a grand ball was about to begin there. "Oh, if only I was made of wax, instead of just plain tallow, I would be glittering now in good society," moaned the little candle. "What possible happiness can be found here? These people have nothing—nothing at all." At that moment the children of the poor family came in to have their supper.

The candle was brought to the table and lighted. The smallest of the poor children reached up and put her arms around the necks of her brother and sister. What she had to tell them was so important that it had to be whispered. "Tonight we're going to have—just think of it—warm potatoes, this very night."

Her face beamed with happiness and the candle beamed right back at her. A gladness filled the candle as it wondered, "Is it such a treat to get warm potatoes? Little children must manage to be happy here, too." And the candle wept tallow tears of joy, and more than that a candle cannot do.

The table was spread and the potatoes were eaten. It was a real feast! There was an apple for everyone, and the smallest child said grace. "And didn't I say it nicely?" the girl asked.

"Don't say such things," her mother told her. "Just thank the good Lord for the food we have this night." The children went to bed, were kissed good night, and fell fast asleep.

"This has been a wonderful evening," the candle said as it burned out. "Could the wax candles have had any better time in their silver candlesticks? I really, really do not think so."

THE SNOW QUEEN

There is, I am told, a king of hobgoblins, and a very wicked, wicked hobgoblin he is. One day, when he was in a most foul mood, he made a looking-glass which had the power of making everything good or beautiful reflected in it almost shrink to nothing, while everything bad or ugly looked huge and more menacing than ever. The most lovely landscapes appeared like boiled spinach, and people became hideous, looking as if they stood on their heads and had no bodies. If a person had even one freckle on their face, it appeared to spread over the whole of their nose and mouth. The hobgoblin found this very amusing. Even when a person had a good or kind thought, the looking-glass could twist it to evil purpose.

All the other hobgoblins talked of its wonders, declaring that people could now, for the first time, see what the world and mankind were really like. The hobgoblins carried the glass about everywhere, till at last there was not a land or a people who had not been looked at through the evil mirror. They wanted even to fly with it up to heaven to see the angels, but the higher they flew the more slippery the glass became, and they could scarcely hold it. At last it slipped from their hands, and fell to the earth, breaking into millions of pieces. But now the looking-glass caused more unhappiness than ever, for the pieces were no larger than a grain of sand, and they flew all about the world. When one of these tiny pieces flew into a person's eye, it remained there unknown to him, and from that moment he saw only the worst in everything he looked at.

Some even got a piece of the mirror in their hearts, and this was most terrible, for their hearts became cold like a lump of ice. Even to this day there are still pieces floating about, but of one piece, which fell long ago, I should like to tell you.

In a large town, full of houses and people, there lived a little boy and a little girl. There names were Kay and Gerda. They lived next door to each other, and one would do nothing without the other. Indeed, their love for each other was so strong, it seemed nothing could come between them. Or so they thought.

It happened one day, as the two children were playing, that Kay was struck by a bit of the magic mirror, not one piece but two; one went into his eye and the other struck his heart, quickly turning it into a lump of ice. They were playing in a garden, and Kay cried out suddenly, "Oh, see! that rose is worm-eaten, and this one is quite crooked. After all they are ugly roses, just like the box in which they stand." And then he kicked the box with his foot, and pulled up the two roses.

"Kay, what are you doing?" cried the little girl.

"I'm doing what pleases me," said Kay. "Oh, don't frown so, it makes you look quite ugly, you know."

From that time on, poor Kay was changed. He told Gerda he had no time for childish games anymore. Everyone thought him quite clever, for he would mimic the speech and walk of the people in the street. Anything disagreeable or strange in a person, Kay could imitate exactly. He would even tease little Gerda, who loved him with all her heart. But it was the glass in his eye, and the coldness in his heart, that made him act like this.

One winter's day, when it snowed, he brought out his sled and went down to the town square to ride with the other boys. In the great square, the boldest boys would tie their sleds to the people's carts, and go with them a good way. While Kay was sledding, a large white sled, pulled by two white horses, rode through the square. Kay tied his little sled behind it, and off they went. The white sled left the square for the countryside, but for some reason, Kay couldn't bring himself to release from the beautiful carriage. Before long, the sled stopped. Snow began to fall, huge flakes, as the driver invited Kay to join her. Kay saw a lady, tall and white. "Are you cold?" she asked, as she kissed him on the forehead. The kiss was colder than ice, and it

went right through his heart. For a moment, he felt as if he would die, but only for a moment; he soon seemed quite well, and thought no more of the cold. She kissed him again, and by this time he had forgotten all about little Gerda, his family, and his home. "Now you must have no more kisses," she said, "or I should kiss you to death."

She was the Snow Queen, ruler of snow and ice. She traveled the wide world, spreading out a blanket of snow as far as the Sun King would allow. Kay looked at her, and saw that she was the most beautiful creature imaginable. To him, she was perfect. The sled suddenly rose in the air and flew north, over a vast expanse of woods and mountains. Below them roared the wild wind; the wolves howled and the snow crackled. Above them shone the moon, clear and bright—and so Kay passed through the long winter's night, and by day he slept at the feet of the Snow Queen.

Nobody knew where Kay went. Many tears were shed for him, and little Gerda wept bitterly for a long time. She knew he must be dead, or surely he would return to her. Oh, that was a long, dreary winter. But at last spring came, with warm sunshine. "Kay is dead and gone," said little Gerda.

"I don't believe it," said the sunshine.

"He is dead and gone," she said to the sparrows.

"We don't believe it," they replied; and Gerda began to doubt it herself. She ran back to her house and gathered up her new red shoes, and then went straightaway to the river.

"Have you taken my little playmate away from me?" she asked the river. "I will give you my new red shoes if you will give him back to me." And it seemed as if the waves nodded to her in a strange manner. Then she took the red shoes, which she liked better than anything else, and threw them in the river. But the shoes washed back near shore, and Gerda had to crawl into a little boat to reach them. As she tried to catch the shoes to throw them further out in the river, the boat came untied and began to float downstream. Without an oar, little Gerda was helpless, and soon she floated far from the town and out into the vast countryside.

At last the little boat came to shore. Gerda jumped out on the bank and found she was in a beautiful garden of flowers. Gerda asked the roses, "Tell me where my Kay has gone?" But the roses just spoke of themselves and nothing more. Then Gerda asked the buttercups, and the tiger-lilies, and the daisies. All told very pretty stories, but of Kay they said nothing. It was no use asking the flowers, for they only knew their own songs. Then the sun beamed down and beckoned to little Gerda, saying, "Little Kay is where I am not. Find the place where my warmth reaches least, and there you shall find your playmate." Gerda didn't understand, but the sunbeam would say nothing more.

"I know, I know where Kay is!" came a screeching voice from behind. Turning, Gerda saw a large crow perched on a branch. "Oh, please, please, tell me!" begged the little girl. "Gently, gently, my child," said the crow. "Your Kay is very far away. A journey I do not advise you to take."

"I don't care how far it is," pleaded Gerda. "I must find Kay. Tell me, please!"

"If you must go," said the crow, "I will go with you. Kay is far to the north, at the very top of the world. Come, and follow me." And the crow flew up and headed north. Little Gerda quickly followed.

The two traveled north all through the spring and summer, and as autumn was coming to a close, they found themselves on the outer reaches of the most northerly clime. There, the snow never melts, and the cold wind never ceases its merciless attack. Little Gerda had suffered a lot along the journey, but her biggest challenge lay ahead.

As she made her way slowly through the ice and snow, Gerda was suddenly set upon by a band of robbers. Grabbing hold of her, an old robber-woman laughed, saying, "She is fat and pretty. She is as good as a little lamb; how nice she will taste!" And as she said this, she drew forth a shining knife, which glittered horribly. "Oh!" screamed the old woman in the next moment; for her own daughter, who held her back, had bitten her on the ear.

"She shall play with me," said the little robber-girl; "she shall give me her muff and her pretty dress, and sleep with me in my bed." Then she bit her mother again, for she was a wild and naughty girl, and all of the robbers laughed.

Gerda was taken to the robber's castle, though she pleaded that they let her go. The crow followed. "You shall sleep with me and all my little animals tonight," said the robber-girl. So she took Gerda down a hall and into a room, where some straw and carpets were laid down. Above them, on perches, were more than a hundred pigeons, who all seemed to be asleep. "These all belong to me. And here is my old sweetheart, Ba." And she dragged out a reindeer by the horns. He wore a bright copper ring round his neck, and was tied up. "We have to hold him tight, or else he would run away from us. I tickle his neck every evening with my sharp knife, which frightens him very much." Gerda thought this horrid, and wondered if the robber-girl would do the same to her.

But as the days passed, Gerda and the little robber-girl became friends. Gerda's goodness actually began to make the robber-girl behave better. Well, a little anyway. Yet, all Gerda could think or talk of, was Kay. One day the crow came to her, saying, "The pigeons have seen little Kay. He is at the palace of the Snow Queen, she who brings snow and ice to the world. Ask the reindeer, he must know where her palace lies."

"Oh, yes," said the reindeer, "it is a glorious place. There is always snow and ice, and you can leap and run about freely on sparkling ice plains." Gerda wept with joy, and ran to the little robber-girl, begging to be released to find her Kay.

"Stop that crying, it makes you look ugly," said the robber-girl. "Oh, very well, you can go. I was getting tired of you, anyway." In truth, the robber-girl was very sad to see Gerda go.

"Take my reindeer, Ba, with you, or you will never make it that far north."

The robber-girl gave Gerda two loaves of bread and a ham, and then cut the rope with which the reindeer was fastened. "Now run, but mind you take good care of the little girl." Gerda climbed on the back of the reindeer, and off they went. The reindeer flew through the snow and ice, and it was but two days when they reached the ice palace of the Snow Queen.

The Snow Queen was away to the south, spreading her icy touch with the first days of winter. Little Kay was left behind, and he sat in the middle of a frozen lake, playing an icy game of reason. He had blocks of ice that he cut to form letters. He sat still and stiff, forming different words. But there was one word he never could manage to form, although he wished it very much. It was the word "Eternity." The Snow Queen had said to him, "When you can find out this, you shall be your own master, and I will give you the whole world and a new pair of skates." But he could not accomplish it.

Gerda ran to him, crying, "Kay, dear little Kay, I have found you at last!" But he sat quite still, stiff, and cold.

Then little Gerda wept hot tears, which fell on his breast, and penetrated into his heart, thawing the lump of ice and washing away the piece of evil glass stuck there. Then he looked at her, and burst into tears, washing away the other evil glass in his eye. He looked around him, and said, "How cold it is, and how large and empty it all looks." Gerda laughed, and then hugged him as she wept with joy.

"Let's go home, Kay," she said.

"Yes, at once," little Kay replied. But before leaving, he quickly bent down and arranged the ice blocks to form a word. Then, taking Gerda's hand, they left. The Snow Queen might come home now when she pleased, for there stood his certainty of freedom, in the word she wanted, written in shining letters of ice.

SOUP FROM A SAUSAGE SKEWER

*I*n a little kingdom, a kingdom of mice, a very very long time ago, there was held a feast. And what a grand feast it was. Everything was first rate. Moldy bread, tallow candles, and sausages were all served in large portions. There was much joking and fun after dinner, with everyone being quite sociable. Nothing was left but the sausage skewers, and this formed the subject of conversation. One mouse reminded the others of an old proverb, 'Soup from a sausage skewer.' Everyone had heard the proverb, but no had ever tasted the soup, much less prepared it. Then the old mouse-king had an idea. He promised that the young lady-mouse who should learn how best to prepare this much talked about and savory soup would be his queen. A year and a day was allowed to discover the secret of the soup. Four young and lively lady-mice took up the challenge, and each was to visit one of the four corners of the world. They each took a sausage skewer as a traveler's staff, and to remind them of the object of their journey.

A year and a day passed, and at the appointed time, the mouse-king called for them. Only three had returned. They gathered in the royal kitchen, and the three lady-mice stood in a row before the mouse-king, while a sausage skewer, covered in black, was placed for the fourth. The king asked each in turn to tell her story. And this is what they had to say.

"When I went out into the world," said the first mouse, "I fancied, as so many my age do, that I already knew everything. But it was not so. I set out by ship on the wide sea, and after many days and nights being chased by the ship's cook, I arrived in a very strange and beautiful land. I found other mice, who took me deep into a forest. The idea that soup could be made from a sausage skewer was to them such an out-of-the-way, unlikely thought, they declared it an impossibility.

"But it was not long before I met those who truly knew of the world, and spoke of things gentle and beautiful. On the edge of the wood, the moon threw its beams particularly on one spot where stood a tree covered with fine moss. All at once I saw the most charming little people marching towards me. They did not reach higher than my knee; yet they looked like humans. Their clothes were very delicate, for they were made of the leaves of flowers. They called themselves elves.

"When they saw me, they cried out 'Maypole, maypole!' and begged to borrow my sausage skewer for their dances. Little spiders spun silvery webs around it, and then the elves began a dazzling dance. And to my surprise, music rose up from my sausage skewer; a glorious sound like a thousand tiny glass bells. My sausage peg was a complete peal of bells. I could scarcely believe that so much beauty could be produced from it. I was so much affected that I wept tears such as a little mouse can weep, but they were tears of joy.

"As morning dawned, the little elves returned my skewer and asked if there was anything they could do for me. I begged them to tell me how to make soup from a sausage skewer."

At this time the mouse-king spoke: "And did they tell you the recipe for the soup?"

The little mouse set her sausage skewer down before the mouse-king, and sounds began to rise from the wooden peg. Soon, everyone could here pots boiling and bubbling with a brew, and the vapory song of a tea-pot filled the air. There was the clanging of pots and pan and the crackling of kitchen fires, all of which was very pleasant to hear.

"What is this?" asked the mouse-king.

"It's what called an 'effect', your majesty," the little mouse said. "Nothing more can my skewer do."

"That is a strange sort of soup," said the mouse-king, "and not very filling, except for one's ears. We shall be glad to hear what information the next may have to give us."

"I was born in a library, at a castle," said the second lady-mouse. "Very few members of our family ever had the good fortune to get into the dining-room, much less the kitchen. We often suffered great hunger, but then we gained a great deal of knowledge. My grandmother said she had heard at one time, for she cannot read, that it was written, 'Those who are poets can make soup of sausage skewers.'

"She then asked me if I was a poet. I said I really did not know. Then she said that the three things necessary to become a poet are understanding, imagination, and feeling. 'If you can manage to acquire these three, you will be a poet, and the sausage-skewer soup will be quite easy to you.'

"In order to gain these all important requirements to become a poet, I knew I had to digest a great deal of writing. I began with the quill pen, soaking the feather in water till it was soft enough to eat. It was very heavy and tough, but I managed to nibble it up at last. It is not so easy to nibble one's self into a poet. I knew there were novels whose sole and only purpose appeared to be that they might relieve mankind of overflowing tears—a kind of sponge, in fact, for sucking up feelings and emotions. I proceeded to devour these books, that is, properly speaking, the interior pages and the binding within. Then I ate a large history, which was quite dry in taste and made my belly ache. Finally, I nibbled a bit more on the romance novels, and something inside me stirred. I knew I had become a poet.

"All my thoughts ran on skewers, sticks of wood, and staves; and as I am, at last, a poet, and I have worked terribly hard to make myself one, I can of course make poetry on anything. I shall therefore be able to wait upon you every day in the week with a poetical history of a skewer. And that is my soup."

"In that case," said the mouse-king, coughing, "we will hear what the third mouse has to say."

"Squeak, squeak," cried a little mouse at the kitchen door. It was the fourth mouse, who everyone thought was dead. She shot in like an arrow, overturning the sausage peg with the

black drape. She had lost her skewer, but not her voice; for she began to speak at once. She had come in so suddenly that no one had time to stop her, so she spoke before the third mouse.

"I started off by train to a large town, but upon my arrival, I was carried away to jail, for I had apparently been hiding in stolen goods. When I arrived at the jail, I overheard the jailers taking about their prisoner. He had been writing and speaking out against something or somebody, I'm not sure which. Anyway, one jailer said, 'The whole affair is like making soup out of sausage skewers, but the soup may cost him his neck.'

"Now this raised an interest in me, so when I had a chance I slipped into his cell. He was writing verse on the cell wall with chalk, but I did not read it. I think he found his time in jail lonely, as he saw me as a welcomed guest. He fed me cheese and bread, and spoke gentle words to me, that soon I really began to love him. He let me run about his hand and into his sleeves, and he called me his little friend. Before long, I forgot all about the sausage skewer and only wished to stay with him always. I stayed, but he did not. He spoke to me so sadly for the last time, and gave me double as much bread and cheese as usual. Then he blew me a kiss with his hand, and they took him away. I do not know what happened to him.

"Sadly, I began my journey back. One night, as I took shelter in a barn along the way, I met up with a lady-owl. She was a clever old owl, and I knew her intent was to eat me. But she was wise in many things, and fond of talk, so I asked her to please tell me how to make soup from a sausage skewer.

"'Soup from a sausage skewer,' she said, 'is only a saying among mankind, and may be understood in many ways. Each believes his own way is best, and after all, the saying means nothing—nothing at all.'

"I managed to escape her clutches to bring you this truth. Truth is not always agreeable, but truth is above everything else, and must be more valuable than soup from a sausage skewer. Your Majesty, the mice are an enlightened people, and the

mouse-king is above them all. He is capable of making me queen for the sake of truth."

"Your truth is a falsehood," said the lady-mouse who had not yet spoken; "I can prepare soup, and I mean to do so."

"I did not travel," said the third mouse; "I stayed right at home and thought hard about the problem. And here is how you prepare soup from a sausage skewer." She set a kettle on the fire and filled it with water right up to the brim. Then she made the fire into a good blaze, keeping it burning till the water began to boil over.

"There, now I throw in the skewer. Will the mouse-king be pleased now to dip his tail into the boiling water, and stir it round. The longer the king stirs it, the stronger the soup will become. Nothing more is necessary, only to stir it."

"Can no one else do this?" asked the king.

"No," said the mouse; "only in the tail of the mouse-king is this power contained."

The mouse-king stood close to the kettle. But he only just touched the hot steam with his tail, when he sprang away from the kettle, exclaiming, "Oh, certainly, by all means, you must be my queen; and we will let the soup question rest till our golden wedding, fifty years from now. That way, the poor in the kingdom can have plenty to eat then, and will have something to look forward to for a long time, with great joy."

And very soon the wedding took place. Many of the mice, as they were returning home, said that the soup could not be properly called "soup from a sausage skewer," but "soup from a mouse's tail."

When the story was spread all over the world, the opinions upon it were divided; but the story remained the same. And, after all, the best way in everything you do, great as well as small, is to expect no thanks for anything you may do, even when it refers to "soup from a sausage skewer."

THE EMPEROR'S NEW CLOTHES

Many years ago there was an Emperor who was so very fond of new clothes that he spent all his money on them. He cared nothing about his soldiers, nor for the theater, nor for riding in the woods except for the sake of showing off his new clothes. He had a costume for every hour in the day. Instead of saying as one does about any other king or emperor, "He is in his council chamber," the people here always said, "The Emperor is in his dressing room."

Life was very gay in the great town where he ruled. Hosts of strangers came to visit it every day, and among them one day were two swindlers. They told everyone that they were weavers and said that they knew how to weave the most beautiful cloth imaginable. Not only were the colors and patterns very fine, but the clothes that were made of this cloth had the peculiar quality of becoming invisible to every person who was not fit for the office he held, or who was impossibly dull.

"Those must be splendid clothes," thought the Emperor. "By wearing them I should be able to discover which men in my kingdom are not fit for their posts. I shall distinguish the wise men from the fools. Yes, I certainly must order some of this cloth to be woven for me."

The Emperor paid the two swindlers a lot of money in advance, so that they might begin their work at once.

They did put up two looms and pretended to weave, but they had nothing whatsoever upon their shuttles. They asked for a quantity of the finest silk and the purest gold thread, all of which they put into their own bags while they worked away at the empty looms far into the night.

"I should like to know how those weavers are getting on with their cloth," thought the Emperor, but he felt a little uneasy when he reflected that anyone who was stupid or unfit for his post would not be able to see it. He certainly thought that he need have no fears for himself, but still he thought he would send somebody else first to see how it was getting on. Everybody in the town knew what wonderful power the cloth possessed, and everyone was anxious to see how stupid his neighbor was.

"I will send my faithful old minister to the weavers," thought the Emperor. "He will be best able to see how the cloth looks, for he is a clever man and no one fulfills his duties better than he does."

So the good old minister went into the room where the two swindlers sat working at the empty looms.

"Heaven help us," thought the old minister, opening his eyes very wide. "Why, I can't see a thing!" But he took care not to say so.

Both the swindlers begged him to be good enough to step a little nearer, and asked if he did not think it a good pattern and beautiful coloring. They pointed to the empty looms. The poor old minister stared as hard as he could, but could not see anything, for of course there was nothing to see.

"Good heavens," thought he. "Is it possible that I am a fool? I have never thought so, and nobody must know it. Am I not fit for my post? It will never do to say that I cannot see this cloth."

"Well, sir, you don't say anything about the cloth," said the one who was pretending to weave.

"Oh, it is beautiful—quite charming," said the minister, looking through his spectacles. "Such a pattern and such colors! I will certainly tell the Emperor that the cloth pleases me very much."

"We are delighted to hear you say so," said the swindlers, and then they named all the colors and described the peculiar pattern. The old minister paid great attention to what they said, so as to be able to repeat it when he got home to the Emperor.

Then the swindlers went on to demand more money, more

silk, and more gold, so they could go on with the weaving. But they put it all into their own pockets. Not a single strand was ever put into the loom. They went on as before, pretending to weave fine cloth.

The Emperor soon sent another faithful official to see how the cloth was getting on and if it would soon be ready. The same thing happened to him as to the minister. He looked and looked, but as there were only the empty looms, he could see nothing at all.

"Is not this a beautiful piece of cloth?" said both the swindlers, showing and explaining the beautiful pattern and colors which were not there to be seen.

"I know I am no fool," thought the man, "so it must be that I am unfit for my good post. It is very strange, though. However, one must not let it appear." So he praised the cloth he did not see, and assured them of his delight in the beautiful colors and the originality of the design.

"It is absolutely charming," he said to the Emperor. Everybody in the town was talking about this most splendid cloth.

Now the Emperor thought he would like to see it while it was still on the looms. So, accompanied by a number of selected courtiers, among whom were the two faithful officials who had already seen the imaginary cloth, he went to visit the crafty imposters. They were working away as hard as ever at the empty looms.

"It is magnificent," said both the honest officials. "Only see, Your Majesty, what a design! What colors!" And they pointed to the empty looms, for they each thought no doubt the others could see the cloth.

"What?" thought the Emperor. "I see nothing at all. This is terrible! Am I a fool? Am I not fit to be emperor? Why, nothing worse could happen to me!"

"Oh, it is beautiful," said the Emperor. "It has my highest approval." And he nodded his satisfaction as he gazed at he empty looms. Nothing would induce him to say that he could

not see anything.

The whole group gazed and gazed, but saw nothing more than all the others. However, they all exclaimed with His Majesty, "It is very beautiful." And they advised him to wear a suit made of this wonderful cloth on the occasion of a great procession which was just about to take place.

"Magnificent! Gorgeous! Excellent!" went from mouth to mouth. They were all equally delighted with it. The Emperor gave each of the rogues an order of knighthood to be worn in their buttonholes and the title of "Gentleman Weaver."

The swindlers sat up the whole night before the day of the procession, burning sixteen candles, so that people might see how anxious they were to get the Emperor's new clothes ready. They cut it out in the air with a huge pair of scissors, and they stitched away with needles without any thread in them.

At last they said, "Now the Emperor's new clothes are ready."

"See, these are the trousers. This is the coat. Here is the mantle," and so on went the crooks as they explained each piece of clothing to the Emperor. "It is as light as a spider's web. One might think one had nothing on, but that is the very beauty of it."

"Yes, I see," said the Emperor.

"Will your Imperial Majesty be graciously pleased to take off your clothes?" said the impostors. "Then we may put on the new ones, along here before the great mirror."

The Emperor took off his clothes, and the impostors pretended to give him one article of dress after another. They then pretended to fasten something around his waist and to tie on something. This was the train, and the Emperor turned round and round in front of the mirror.

"How well His Majesty looks in the new clothes! How becoming they are!" cried all the people round. "What a design, and what colors! They are most gorgeous robes."

"Everything is ready for Your Majesty to begin the procession," said the master of the ceremonies.

"Well, I am quite ready," said the Emperor. "Don't the clothes fit well?" Then he turned round again in front of the mirror, so that he should seem to be looking at his grand things.

The chamberlains who were to carry the train stooped and pretended to lift if from the ground with both hands, and they walked along with their hands in the air. They dared not let it appear that they could not see anything.

Then the Emperor walked along in the procession, and everybody in the streets and at the windows exclaimed, "How beautiful the Emperor's new clothes are! What a splendid train! And they fit to perfection!"

Nobody would let it appear that he or she could see nothing, for then they would not be fit for their post, or else they were fools. None of the Emperor's clothes had been so successful before.

"But he has got nothing on," said a little child.

"Oh, listen to the innocent," said the father. And one person whispered to the other what the child had said. "He has nothing on—a child says he has nothing on!"

"But he has nothing on!" at last cried all the people.

The Emperor blushed bright red, for he knew it was true. But he thought, "The procession must go on now." So he held himself stiffer than ever, and the chamberlains held up the invisible train.